MILE END

To urban kids around the world who illuminate
concrete alleys with their brimming imaginations,
starting with Arnaud and Florent, my own
two Mile Enders and inspiration

Special thanks to my friend and agent, Kirsten Hall, whose sense
of wonder and intuition guided me toward this adventure

All rights reserved. Published in the United States by Random House Children's Books,
a division of Penguin Random House LLC, New York. Published simultaneously in Canada
by Tundra Books, Toronto, in 2017.

Random House and the colophon are registered trademarks of Penguin Random House LLC.

Visit us on the Web! randomhousekids.com

Educators and librarians, for a variety of teaching tools, visit us at RHTeachersLibrarians.com

Library of Congress Cataloging-in-Publication Data is available upon request.

ISBN 978-0-553-53659-1 (trade) — ISBN 978-0-553-53660-7 (lib. bdg.) —
ISBN 978-0-553-53661-4 (ebook)

MANUFACTURED IN CHINA

10 9 8 7 6 5 4 3 2 1

First American Edition

Edited by Tara Walker and Maria Modugno
Designed by Isabelle Arsenault and Kelly Hill
The artwork in this book was rendered in pencils, watercolor, and ink
with digital coloration in Photoshop.
Hand-lettering by Isabelle Arsenault

A Mile End Kids Story

COLETTE'S LOST PET

Words and pictures by
ISABELLE ARSENAULT

Random House New York

No, Colette!
For the last time, NO PET!
Now go explore your new
neighborhood.

Hey, Lily!

Have you seen
Colette's lost pet?
It's a parakeet.

Gee, that's not the kind of bird I usually see around here. What color is it?

Um, well...

uhhh... It's blue!

With a bit of yellow on its neck.

Hey, Scott!

Have you seen Colette's lost pet? It's a parakeet. It's blue with a bit of yellow on its neck.

Oh, what's
its name?

Um,
well . . .

uh . . . Marie.

Marie-Antoinette!
Like the princess.

Hey, Maya!

Prrrr
uiiiii

Have you seen Colette's lost pet?
It's a parakeet. It's blue with a
bit of yellow on its neck, and its
name is Marie-Antoinette.

What does it
sound like?

Um, well . . . uh . . .

Like PRrrrrrr
Prrrr PrrrrrruiiiiiiT!

And it speaks a
little bit, too.

But only
in French.

Bien sûr!

Aw, cute!
I haven't heard it
but I did hear
Beth's cat meowing.
It passed by just
a minute ago . . . .

Oh!

To Beth's!

Don't worry, Colette.
We'll find Marie-Annette!

Marie-Antoinette!

Hey, Beth!

Have you seen Colette's lost pet?
It's a parakeet. It's blue with a bit
of yellow on its neck, its name is
Marie-Antoinette and it makes
a sound like PRrrrrrr
Prrrr PrrrrrruiiiiiiT!

I don't think so.
Do you have a picture
of it?

Um, well . . .

uh . . .

Too bad I don't
have that great shot
we took in . . .

uh, Hawaii.

I can draw it
though!

Hey, Lukas!

ave you seen Colette's lost pet? It's a parakeet. It's blue with a bit of yellow on its neck, its name is Marie-Antoinette, it makes a sound like PRrrrrrr Prrrr Prrrrrruiiiiiit and it SURFS! See this drawing? Can you help us make it into a poster?

Let me see.
Is this your bird's
actual size?

Um, well . . . uh . . .

yes, pretty much,
I guess.

But . . .

Until it became TOO BIG to fit in the house!

But then it was the perfect size to fly around!

So we traveled the world.

We flew to Paris . . .
and Japan!

Bien sûr!

We've been to
the desert . . .

and sailed
the sea.

And we ate a
rattlesnake in the jungle!

I'm telling you,
this parakeet is <u>truly</u>
amazing!

It's just the best pet you could ever dream of ...

and it's MINE!

Colette!

Um . . . well, okay!

I'll tell you more later!

Can't wait!

Hey, tomorrow let's explore the jungle!

You bet! I'd love that!

CLARK ALLEY